D0341318

# Stitch Head

## The Pirate's Eye

To Mum and Dad
~Guy Bass


For Alice Ballard
a book for big school!
~Pete Williamson

Bass, Guy.
The pirate's eye /

2013.
3370507050005
cu                07/11/14

# STITCH HEAD

## The Pirate's Eye

# GUY BASS

### ILLUSTRATED BY
## PETE WILLIAMSON

capstone
young readers

# A FOREWORD OF
# WARNING
## (in the form of a rousing old sea song sung by salty sea dogs)

*When the seas be rough and the waves be quick,*
*Yo ho ho and slap your thigh!*
*There's only one sailor who isn't sick,*
*Ahoy! Captain Flashpowder!*

*The waves do crash with brutish clout,*
*Yo ho ho and spit in your eye!*
*But steady sails the Gadabout,*
*Ahoy! Captain Flashpowder!*

*The captain hunts for long-lost gold —*
*Yo ho ho and tickle your toes!*
*He'll be rich afore he's old,*
*Ahoy! Captain Flashpowder!*

*His eagle eye looks out to sea —*
*Yo ho ho and pick your nose!*
*He goes o'er the edge if he wants a wee,*
*Ahoy! Captain Flashpowder!*

WELCOME TO
# GRUBBERS NUBBIN
(POPULATION 665)
## YESTERYEAR

# ALMOST-LIFE AND TIMES

## (The shadow of Castle Grotteskew)

*"Onward, to Adventure!*
*Via Excitement!"*

From
*The Daring Diary of*
*Captain Flashpowder*

I was the night that everything changed. The circus had come to Grubbers Nubbin.

Yesteryear! What a wonderful time it was. Yesteryear was filled with song and cheer, with funny hats and mustaches and horses pulling carts, with cobbled streets and expressions like "Lawks-a-mussy!" and "Hooken-snivey!" Yes, all in all, yesteryear was just about the best time to be alive.

Unless you lived in the small town of Grubbers Nubbin, that is. For in Grubbers Nubbin, even on the brightest day, a dark shadow fell upon the town. The shadow of CASTLE GROTTESKEW.

High on a hill above the town loomed the castle. It had loomed there since before anyone could remember. The castle was home to the maddest of mad professors, Mad Professor Erasmus. For more years than it is possible to count on four people's fingers, the professor had busied himself creating hundreds of monstrous, unearthly creatures.

The very first of his monstrous creations was a small, almost-human creature that the professor had named STITCH HEAD.

Stitch Head was a jigsaw of bits, pieces, and spare parts. His bald and round head was covered with stitches, and his eyes were different colors. One eye was black and boring, but the other was a bright, ice-blue orb. It shined like the ocean on a cloudless morning.

Long forgotten by his master, Stitch Head spent his days hiding in the darkest shadows of the castle, silently watching over the professor and his many creations. Fortunately, the castle's inhabitants rarely caused trouble. After all, they were some of the nicest monsters you could ever meet.

But they rarely started out that way.

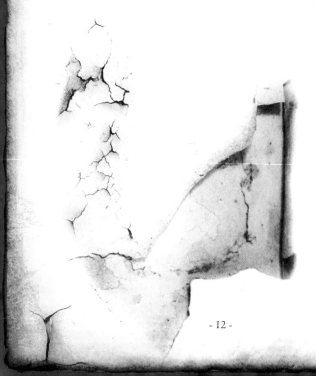

# THE ROOT OF ALL EVIL

## (We're going to need a bigger dose)

> *"You haven't seen the world until you've seen it through a pirate's eye."*
>
> From
> *The Daring Diary of Captain Flashpowder*

"R<small>UN!</small>"

Stitch Head raced down the moonlit corridor, his mismatched eyes flashing with fear. He had a small bag slung over his shoulder, which clanked and clinked as he ran. In his tiny hand he gripped an ink-blue bottle.

"Empty . . ." he whispered — and looked behind him.

"Oh . . . oh, no," he said. "It's here!"

A strange-looking, three-armed creature appeared from the gloom, stampeding after him. It was a hulking, beastly thing with a terrifying combination of monstrously strange parts. It charged along the corridor, gaining on Stitch Head with every step. Then, when it was almost upon him, its ear-piercing roar filled the air . . .

"WAAA-AAAHH! Faster, Stitch Head! It's going to EAT us to PIECES!" cried the Creature.

Stitch Head and the Creature both glanced back. Behind them, in the dim light of the corridor, emerged another monster. It was huge — five times bigger than the Creature, and an impossible combination of octopus, sea snake, squid, and upside-down-faced horribleness. It writhed its way toward them, roaring and screeching so loudly that it cracked the castle walls.

"*GRREEOOORRGH!*"

"I thought your POTION was meant to CURE it of its monstrousness!" cried the Creature (it still hadn't chosen a name for itself, so it was just called the Creature).

"It was!" cried Stitch Head, searching in his potion bag as he tore down the corridor. "We're going to need a bigger dose!"

"What do you think it's so GRUMPY about, anyway? It's only been almost-alive for FIVE WHOLE MINUTES . . ." cried

the Creature. "Maybe it didn't WANT to be brought to almost-life."

"It's the Root of All Evil!" panted Stitch Head, as the shadow of the octo-monster loomed over them. "The professor has been growing the root in his laboratory . . . he must have added it to his creation! It's made it . . . *bad*. I thought my Serenity Salve would cure it, but —"

# "GRREEEOOORGH!"

The tentacled octo-monster launched itself toward them with all its crazed might. Stitch Head and the Creature leaped aside as the beast crashed through the floor, plummeting to the level below.

The Creature dusted itself off and peered though the hole left by the octo-monster. "Well, THAT was a stroke of LUCK," it said.

A moment later, the remains of the ancient floor crumbled beneath their feet. Stitch Head and the Creature plunged to the lower level with an "AAAAH!" and a cascade of rubble.

## THE SECOND CHAPTER

# ENTER ARABELLA

### (A brand-new pair of kicking boots)

*"Free treasure!
What a steal!"*

From
*The Daring Diary of
Captain Flashpowder*

"Creature?" whimpered Stitch Head, dragging himself to his feet. He looked around, but all he could see was rubble. Where was it? "Creature? Are you there?"

A vast, dark shadow fell over Stitch Head. He heard a deep, rumbling growl and felt hot breath on the back of his head.

"Uh-oh . . ." he said in a tiny, frightened whisper. He turned slowly to see the octo-monster looming over him.

# "GREOOORGH!"

The octo-monster roared in Stitch Head's face, almost knocking him over with the force and foulness of its breath. Stitch Head stared into the beast's mouth, frozen with fear. This was the end. Silvery drool dripped from the octo-monster's hundred-toothed jaws as it closed in.

"Hey! Snot-breath! Don't make me come down there and smash your nose in!" came a cry. The octo-monster whirled round and looked up at the hole in the ceiling. There, standing on the edge, was a thin, scruffy-looking girl.

"Arabella . . ." whispered Stitch Head, peering up.

Arabella was a girl from Grubbers Nubbin and, apart from the professor, was the only human being Stitch Head could call his friend.

Unlike the other townsfolk, Arabella couldn't get enough of the monsters, creatures, and crazy things in Castle Grotteskew. In fact, Stitch Head was pretty sure she wasn't scared of anything.

Even if she was about to be eaten.

"Arabella, get out of here!" shouted Stitch Head. "RUN!"

"GREOOAAAEEGH!"

The octo-monster reared up to its full height. Its tentacles were flailing wildly.

But Arabella didn't move an inch. She just shook her head and pointed to her shoes.

"You see these?" said Arabella. "These are my brand-new kicking boots. They're polished up all nice and shiny, so you'll be able to see your face in them when I kick it in!"

The octo-monster slithered up the wall and launched itself through the hole with another rage-filled scream.

The octo-monster wrapped one of its tentacles around Arabella and held her over the hole.

"ARABELLA!" screamed Stitch Head. "Hang on!"

"I'll kick you into next week!" she growled, as the octo-monster gnashed its jaws.

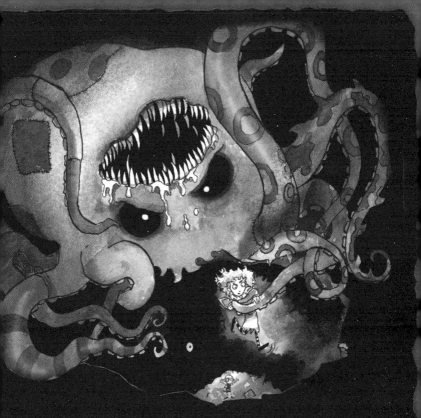

"GREO . . . ooR . . . GReorhh . . .
uhhhg . . . ?" the octo-monster gurgled.

Suddenly, the monster shook its head
and rubbed its huge, black eyes with two of
its tentacles.

"My dear child, I must apologize for
such improper behavior on my part," it said
in a soft, eerily polite tone. "I cannot for
the almost-life of me imagine what could

have prompted such abominable conduct! Although I confess I don't remember anything at all — even my own *name*. I must *choose* one — being nameless feels quite improper."

Creature sighed. "TELL me about it," he said.

"The Serenity Salve," whispered Stitch Head. "It's working . . ."

"Yeah, well, count yourself lucky," huffed a disappointed Arabella. "I was just about to get kicky all over your face."

"Then I am profoundly grateful I came to my senses when I did," said the octo-monster, lowering Arabella through the hole and placing her delicately on the ground.

"Now, if you'll be kind enough to allow me to take my leave, I suddenly feel rather dehydrated," continued the octo-monster. "Is there by chance a body of water nearby in which I might take up residence? As you can see, I do not have a home."

"There's . . . um, there's a moat around the castle," said Stitch Head. "You can get to it through the sewer pipes — that is, if you can squeeze through them . . ."

"A fantastic suggestion! My humblest thanks to you," said the octo-monster. "And if I can ever be of assistance — anything at all — just give me a whistle!"

With that, the giant octo-monster slid into the shadows of Castle Grotteskew and disappeared.

"I don't even know if I *can* whistle . . ." muttered Stitch Head.

"Too bad I scared him off," grumbled Arabella. "Would've been nice to try out my new boots."

"Uh, I think it was the Serenity Sal — um, never mind," said Stitch Head quietly. "Thanks for . . . wait, where's the Creature? Creature! Creature, where are you —?"

"That was GREAT!" boomed the Creature, clambering out from under a mound of rubble. "I haven't FALLEN through a HOLE on my HEAD in WEEKS. It really clears out the COBWEBS. Hi, Arabella! I like your BOOTS! But HOW did you get into the CASTLE?"

"I got my own key made," replied Arabella, showing off a large key around her neck. "Good thing too. That monster was going to swallow Stitch Head like a pickled egg. So, have you thought of a name for yourself yet?"

"I've narrowed it DOWN," boomed the Creature excitedly. "Do you want to hear the SHORTLIST? I'll start with the A's: ABRAHAM, ALBATROSS, ALBERT, ALFRED, ALGERNON, ALVIN, ANGELA, ANGELINA, ANGELO, ANTELOPE, ARCHIBALD, ARTHUR —"

"Yikes, Creature, I'll be older than my grandma by the time you get to the Z's — and my grandma's so old that her toenails have fallen off!" said Arabella, chuckling.

"Hey, where ARE we?" asked the Creature, glancing around. "THIS doesn't look ANYTHING like the rest of the castle."

Stitch Head glanced with his mismatched eyes across the room . . . and froze. "It can't be . . ." he began.

"Are you all right?" asked Arabella. Stitch Head didn't reply. He just stared into the doorway. Arabella waved her hand in front of Stitch Head's face. "Anyone in there? You look like you've seen a ghost."

"I didn't think there WERE any GHOSTS in Castle Grotteskew," said the Creature, panicking. "Should we start RUNNING and SCREAMING now?"

"This is the room," whispered Stitch Head, finally.

"What room?" asked Arabella. "What is this place?"

"This is my master's — the professor's — old playroom," said Stitch Head. "This is where I was created."

# THE THIRD CHAPTER

# THE FORGOTTEN ROOM

## (The Daring Diary of Captain Flashpowder)

*"Tomorrow is just an adventure you haven't had yet."*

From
*The Daring Diary of Captain Flashpowder*

"NO WAY — this is the PROFESSOR's old playroom?" boomed the Creature. The Forgotten Room was like no other in the castle. It wasn't filled with brains in jars or hideous, half-finished creations. There were no chains hanging from the ceiling, or strange creations roaming around. Instead, there were toys — a rocking horse, a bucket

of rusty tin soldiers, a moth-eaten teddy
bear, a train set . . . and mountains of
books, all covered in a thick layer of dust
and cobwebs. In the middle of the room
was the only clue to the professor's
future — a small table attached to a
makeshift electrical generator.

"You were born here?" asked Arabella.

"Well, *made* . . ." said Stitch Head.

"Of COURSE! And you're very well made!" bellowed the Creature reassuringly. "The stitches really bring out the different parts of your FACE."

"That — that's a creating table. It is where my master brought me to almost-life," said Stitch Head, pointing at the table. "This room was my home for years. When my master's father took him away to become a mad professor, I was locked inside. I hoped my master would come back for me . . . but he never did. Eventually, one of his mad monsters rampaged through the castle. It broke down the door and freed me. But by then the castle was full of creations, and I was *forgotten*."

"POOR Stitch Head," whimpered the Creature, wiping away a tear with its third arm.

"You'd better not start crying," groaned Arabella. "Crybabies make me clench my fists."

"I — I wasn't GOING to . . ." replied the Creature with a sniff.

"You know what you need, Stitch Head?" said Arabella, as she started sifting through the piles of books. "You need to get out more."

"That's a GREAT idea!" cried the Creature, who thought almost everything was a great idea. "We should go on a TRIP! We could all go to the BEACH and work on our TANS. I'm such a PALE shade of GRAY these days. . ."

"Leave Grotteskew? We can't! I mean I can't — not ever," said Stitch Head, with a rare determination.

Only once had Stitch Head ventured beyond the castle walls. One dark, foreboding night, a circus ringmaster by the name of Fulbert Freakfinder had come calling at Grotteskew's Great Door, promising Stitch Head fame and fortune as the star of his Traveling Carnival of Unnatural Wonders. For the first time, Stitch Head had considered the possibility that there was something more to almost-life than being forgotten. Indeed, if it weren't for Freakfinder's final betrayal, Stitch Head might have left Castle Grotteskew forever. What would have become of his master then? Who would have cured each new creation of its madness and monstrosity? Stitch Head never forgave himself for his selfishness. From that moment, he had vowed never to leave the castle again.

"I'm sorry, but I can't leave," Stitch Head repeated, wiping the dust from the professor's creating table. "The professor *needs* me."

"Yeah, right . . . needs you to cure all his mad monsters, you mean," quipped

Arabella, as she tossed books over her shoulder. "I'm surprised he ain't better at it, what with all these professoring manuals — there's hundreds of 'em! He should get another hobby, or . . . hang on, what's this?"

She picked up a thick, leather-bound book and blew off the dust. On the cover was a picture of a pirate.

"Who's Captain Flashpowder?" asked Arabella, holding up the book.

Beneath the title was a painting of a heroic-looking figure with an eyepatch. In his hand he wielded a gleaming cutlass sword. He was standing at the stern of a huge ship — a *pirate* ship — and he had a bright red and yellow parrot perched on his shoulder.

"My master *loved* that book," whispered Stitch Head, his ice-blue eye gleaming in the moonlight. "He used to read it to me every night. It's the diary of a great pirate. It tells of his adventures to faraway lands, searching for treasure . . . excitement . . . piracy on the high seas."

"GREAT! I LOVE pirates!" the Creature exclaimed. "HEY, that gives me an IDEA — let's play PIRATES! Oh, can we, PLEASE? All the other creations want to play is TEA PARTIES . . ."

"Stitch Head will have to be Captain Flashpowder," said Arabella, showing the

Creature the diary. "He's already got his eye. Look!"

"Hey, you're RIGHT!" boomed the Creature. "Captain FLUSHPOWDER'S got Stitch Head's eye. I mean, Stitch Head's got HIS! I mean —"

"What . . . what do you mean?" asked Stitch Head. He peered at the diary's cover. Flashpowder's left eye was bright, piercing, almost glimmering — and ice blue.

Arabella chuckled. "Ain't no denying it, Stitch Head — that eye of yours is the absolute same as the pirate's."

"Are . . . are my eyes different from each other?" asked Stitch Head, more than a little embarrassed.

Stitch Head didn't make a habit of looking at his reflection. Seeing himself only reminded him how small and unimpressive he was compared to the other impressive creations in the castle. He had no idea that one of his eyes looked different from the other.

"Stitch Head," said Arabella. "I think it's about time you had a good look at yourself."

# THE FOURTH CHAPTER

# UPON REFLECTION
## (Stitch Head's eye)

*"Keep your eye on the horizon and your poop on the poop deck."*

From
*The Daring Diary
of Captain Flashpowder*

Arabella took a small pocket mirror out of her dress.

"Is that so you can make sure you look NICE and PRETTY all the time?" boomed the Creature.

"No, it's so I can see creatures sneaking up on me," replied Arabella. "Boys like to pull my hair, and I like to smash their teeth in for trying."

"Now REMEMBER, Stitch Head," began the Creature. "There's no SHAME in SCREAMING at your HIDEOUSNESS. I do it ALL the time."

"Stop worrying. I've seen stray dogs uglier than you, Stitch Head," said Arabella, holding out the mirror. "Here, have a look at yourself."

Stitch Head peered into the mirror. He saw his round, worried face staring back at him. The first thing he noticed were his stitches, which ran like tiny train tracks

across his face, separating the pale patches of skin.

"See? Not so bad, is it?" added Arabella.

Stitch Head shrugged. He didn't look as strange as most of the professor's creations, and he certainly didn't feel like screaming. He peered closer. His right eye glinted hypnotically. It was a bright ice blue — and looked *exactly* like Captain Flashpowder's.

"SEE?" hollered the gleeful Creature. "You've got a PIRATE'S EYE! You're part SWASHBUCKLER!"

"But that's not possible . . . is it?" asked Stitch Head. He knew he was made up from spare parts, but he'd never really thought about where they had come from.

Stitch Head sat down on a pile of books. "What does it mean?" he whispered.

"What do you think it means?" said Arabella. "It means the professor somehow got his hands on Flashpowder's diary and

his lost eye — and he gave that eye to you. The Creature's right — you might look like a rag doll that's been run over by a horse . . . but you're definitely part pirate."

That night, with Arabella back home in Grubbers Nubbin and the Creature posing for an almost-life drawing class with some of the other creations, Stitch Head made his way deep into the maze-like bowels of the castle, far from the Forgotten Room, down winding, unlit staircases until he reached the dankest, darkest corner of Castle Grotteskew — the dungeon that he called home.

There, he lay on his bed and opened *The Daring Diary of Captain Flashpowder*. It suddenly felt as if no time had passed since the professor had read it to him back in the playroom.

Zounds abounds!

Here be writ the most daring exploits of I, Captain Dash Flashpowder, the most undaunted pirate ever to set sail upon the seas!

Together with my loyal crew and trusty parrot companion, Pilgrim, I journey the world aboard the good ship Gadabout, in search of hidden treasures, lost islands and voyages to . . .

. . . The Edge of Possibility.

Zounds abounds!

Fix your eye on the horizon and let's set sail.

Onward . . . to adventure!

Stitch Head's mind was racing with possibilities. Could Flashpowder's lost eye really have found its way to Castle Grotteskew, along with his diary? He felt his almost-living heart beat ever faster as he turned the page.

*Captain's chronicle, September 25th. Day 313 aboard my trusty vessel, the* Gadabout.

By my boots! My trusty queen and mistress, the Sea, is as choppy as if a giant squid were rocking the ship with its eight monstrous tentacles! Which is impossible, because I killed that squid last week! Zounds abounds!

Flashpowder: 1, Squid: 0!

But, while the smell of my trusty crew's seasickness grows stronger by the day, so, too, does the smell of buried treasure! (Not literally. Treasure smells not.) For today, my trusty fowl companion, Pilgrim, returned from his flight with gratifying news. He has found land!

At least I think that's what he said. It was mainly squawking. *Squawk! Squawk!* All day, every day . . . One day I shall *strangle* that trusty companion.

Where was I? Oh, yes! Land! Land means treasure . . . treasure means danger . . . danger means adventure.

Avast ye! Hoist the mizzen mast! Splice the mainbrace! Swab the poop deck! By my lonely, gleaming eye, we sail once more to adventure! Via excitement!

"To adventure," repeated Stitch Head.

He closed the book and looked again at the cover, staring into Flashpowder's eye. The resemblance to his own eye was uncanny. Could he really be part pirate? Stitch Head suddenly wondered if he was destined for more than just hiding away in a castle for the rest of his days. After all, shouldn't even a part pirate be out sailing the oceans, looking for lost islands and hidden treasure?

Stitch Head sighed, remembering his promise to his master. He could never leave Castle Grotteskew, not as long as Professor Erasmus called it home.

Still, that was all the more reason to dream. He tried to picture himself aboard the *Gadabout*, the sun warming his skin as he strode up and down the deck. He tried to picture the waves buffeting the ship as he cast his ice-blue eye out to the horizon, to a distant, treasure-filled island. He tried imagining his crew singing bold sea shanties as they swabbed the poop deck. He felt for the sword by his side and held out his arm for the return of his trusty companion.

But the more Stitch Head tried to picture himself as Captain Flashpowder, the more he was reminded of who he really was — a mad professor's small, forgotten creation.

No, if he was going to imagine himself as a pirate . . . he had to *become* a pirate.

# THE FIFTH CHAPTER

# A TRUSTY SWORD

## (Stitch Head looks for his inner pirate)

*"Whoever said the pen
is mightier than the sword
has only ever been stabbed
with a pen."*

From
*The Daring Diary of
Captain Flashpowder*

S titch Head spent the rest of the night making a list of all the really piratey things about the amazing Captain Flashpowder.

A trusty ship

A trusty crew

A trusty companion
(preferably a parrot)

A trusty sword

An ice-blue eye

"An ice-blue eye" didn't seem vital to becoming a pirate, but it was the one thing he and Flashpowder did have in common. All the other stuff seemed pretty hard to come by. Where on earth was he going to get a ship? Or a parrot?

Stitch Head decided to start small. He found a slim piece of wood and carved one end to a point with a not-particularly-sharp rock. Then he found a smaller piece of wood and tied it on near the base with a piece of rope.

"My trusty sword," he said. He began swinging the piece of wood, trying to imagine he was Captain Flashpowder facing a fearsome sea serpent or a horde of hungry ghost-pirates. In the end, it just made him feel like a mad professor's first creation swinging a piece of wood.

With determination, he clambered onto a nearby table and reached up for one of the many chains that hung from the ceiling. He grabbed the chain and leaped into the air, imagining he was swinging from the rigging of the *Gadabout*!

"Afast ye!" he cried in his loudest whisper, as he flew across the dungeon. "Spice the mail brace! Hoist the middle mast! To advent — OOOOF!"

KRUMP!

Stitch Head flew face first into a wall and slid to the ground with a THUD!

"Oww . . ."

He lay motionless for a minute, the sound of the chains still clanging in his ears. Then he checked to see if any of his stitches had come loose and inspected his sword, which had snapped halfway down. He took another piece of rope and tied it around his waist like a belt. Then he hooked in the sword . . . and sighed. He still didn't feel like a pirate — at *all*.

He needed a trusty companion.

# THE SIXTH CHAPTER

# A TRUSTY COMPANION
### (Stitch Head visits the laboratory)

*"A trusty companion
should be brave, fearless,
reliable … and, in case of
emergency, edible."*

From
*The Daring Diary of
Captain Flashpowder*

A fter sunrise, Stitch Head set to work finding himself a trusty companion.

Of course, there was the Creature. It had been Stitch Head's "bestest friend" since the day of its creation, when Stitch Head had cured it of a nasty case of werewolfism. He trusted the Creature more than anyone, but he couldn't exactly keep it perched on his shoulder. No, Stitch Head needed a *parrot*.

His master, Professor Erasmus, had a baffling collection of so-called ingredients for use in his experiments. His laboratory was filled with an extensive store of less-than-alive creatures (or parts of them) from all over the world. Surely he would have a parrot or two lying around.

Over the years, Stitch Head had found a dozen different ways of getting inside the laboratory — and all without being spotted by his master. Until now, he had been looking for ingredients for his cures — the endless potions, tonics, and ointments he'd created to stop his professor's more unpredictable creations from running wild. But today, only a parrot would do.

Stitch Head crawled through a crack in the east wall of the laboratory. It was a huge room with a high ceiling, with plenty of dark shadows in which to hide — even as the light of the morning tried to creep in.

At the far end of the laboratory, the professor was pacing back and forth near his desk. He was clutching a handful of notes and calculations and mumbling things like, "AHA! It needs bigger toes!" and, "How many brains are too many?"

Stitch Head headed for the other end of the room, where the professor kept his vast store of ingredients. Along the far wall was a high, wide tower of wooden shelves, filled with crates, boxes, and jars, each containing things of unimaginable strangeness — and labeled accordingly.

Stitch Head passed by a jar of eyes marked "SLIGHTLY ALIVE EYES — HANDLE WITH STARE." He instinctively looked away as the eyes bobbed about in the yellowish liquid.

"Cat's whiskers . . . dog's breath . . . dragon's teeth . . ." he mumbled, as he moved along the first shelf — jar after jar, bottle after bottle. There was nothing that even resembled a parrot. He clambered up to a higher shelf and began carefully making his way along it.

"Crow's feet . . . owl's brains . . . elephant memory lobes . . ." he muttered, as he shuffled along the shelf. There was still no sign of even a single piece of a parrot. He climbed higher.

By the time he had reached the highest shelf, Stitch Head had almost given up hope.

The shelf itself was rotting and covered in cobwebs, and crammed with dozens of neglected, sad-looking sacks marked "SPARE PARTS." These were the bits and pieces that simply weren't good enough for his master's impressive creations . . . just like the parts the young professor had used to make Stitch Head all those years ago.

But then, at the far end of the shelf, he spotted something glinting in the lamplight — large, dust-covered jar marked "PICKLED PARROT PARTS."

"Perfect!" whispered Stitch Head. "And perfectly *pickled*."

Stitch Head cautiously made his way along the shelf as the ancient, dry wood splintered beneath him. He dared to look down and realized how perilously high he had climbed.

He held his breath and fixed his gaze on the bright colors of the parrot parts. He reached out with his tiny arm, but it was too far away. He shuffled along a bit farther . . . and heard a loud CRRREEEAAK.

"Uh-oh," Stitch Head muttered, as he felt the shelf start to buckle. He stared down in horror to see the wood splinter and crack . . . and the parrot jar begin to slide off the shelf!

Stitch Head grabbed it with both hands, but it was too heavy. For a moment, it was like time stood still.

Stitch Head held on for his almost-life —
and he, the jar and a dozen or so sacks of
spare parts plummeted to the ground!

"AaaaaaAAAH —" Stitch Head cried
out.

# CRRRRASSSSH!

The jar shattered into a thousand shards,
sending pieces of pickled parrot flying
across the laboratory.

Stitch Head panicked. *The professor!* What if he caught his first creation stealing from him?

Stitch Head scrambled to his feet, slipping and sliding in the slick of spilled pickled parrot goo. Then, as he raced for the crack in the wall, he instinctively grabbed one of the sacks of spare parts. He had almost made his escape when he stopped . . . and looked back.

"I know! I'll add another head!" screamed the professor, oblivious to Stitch Head's mishap. "Mad professoring is all about extra heads these days! This will be my greatest creation ever! AHAHA-AHAHAA!"

Stitch Head kicked himself for worrying. His master would not notice him — or the broken jar. All the professor could see was his next creation.

Stitch Head sighed, slung the sack over his shoulder, and disappeared into the shadows.

# STITCH HEAD'S FIRST CREATION
## (Part monkey, part bat)

> "Piracy is a point of view."
>
> From
> *The Daring Diary of
> Captain Flashpowder*

Stitch Head carefully made his way to the Forgotten Room. It was still early and the castle was quiet. The Creature (who was quite the social butterfly) was no doubt regaling the other creations with tales of their octo-monster escapade, so it was the perfect time to work without interruptions.

He emptied the spare parts sack on to the creating table. There was one mostly moldy monkey and a few bits of battered bat . . . hardly the ideal ingredients for a trusty companion.

Stitch Head stared at the parts and began assembling them in his head. He had watched so many of his master's experiments brought to life, it almost seemed like second nature to him. He quickly set to work, toiling all day and all night on his creation.

By the following morning, his trusty companion was ready to be brought to almost-life.

"Here goes nothing," he said to himself,

looking down at the tiny, cobbled-together creature. Stitch Head pumped in the last of the cultivation goo, attached a handful of electrodes and turned on the makeshift generator. It hadn't been used for more than forty years — did it still work? Did it have enough power to bring the creation to almost-life, as it had him? There was only one way to find out.

"Live . . . please," he added, and pulled the life-lever. After a moment, bright blue bolts of electricity darted out of the machine. The creature began to shake uncontrollably and gray smoke poured from its ears.

"Uh, less power? More? What do I do?" cried Stitch Head, his hand gripping the life-lever. Suddenly, the generator began to spark and fizz as if it were coming apart at the seams. The machine started glowing with uncontrolled energy . . .

FTZZZZ-KRKLE-TZZZZ!

# KRAKA-BOOOOM!

The generator exploded! Stitch Head crashed headfirst into a pile of books as shards of sparking metal flew past him! He scrambled to his feet and peered into the thick smoke. Had his creation been blown to bits?

After a moment, something *moved*.

"Hello?" Stitch Head said.

He waved the smoke away with his hands. There, on the floor, sat a small blue and gray creature. He was a strange, unpleasant combination of parts. While he was more or less monkey-shaped, his front legs were the folded wings of a bat, and he also had a bat's wide, flat nose.

The monkey-bat unfolded his wings as if he were trying to remember what they were.

"I — I did it. My first creation! My very own . . . monkey-bat!" whispered Stitch Head. "My trusty companion!"

He knelt down and held out his hand. "It's okay, don't be afraid. I am Stitch Head. I'm your *master*."

The monkey-bat chirped and cocked his head.

Then he bared his teeth . . . and his eyes flooded with rage!

"GRrrrRRRR . . ." the strange creation muttered.

"Uh-oh," said Stitch Head.

# "GRRRAAHHH!"

# I SHALL CALL HIM . . . POX!

## (Arabella saves the day again)

> *"Just because I'm stealing
> from you, doesn't mean
> we can't be friends!"*
>
> From
> *The Daring Diary of
> Captain Flashpowder*

As it turned out, Stitch Head's first
creation was also the most vicious,
monstrous creature he had ever met — and
that was really saying something. After all
but destroying the Forgotten Room, the
tiny monkey-bat flew into the castle. Stitch
Head barely escaped with his stitches intact.
He hurried down to his dungeon home and
gathered all the calming curatives, soothing
salves, and treating tonics he could cram
into his bag.

As Stitch Head raced out of the dungeon,
the monkey-bat was already rampaging
through the castle. Stitch Head simply
followed the terrified screams of the castle's
other creations to discover the whereabouts
of his so-called trusty companion.

Before long, Stitch Head found himself
in the most populated part of the castle.
He rarely ventured this far. He had yet
to introduce himself to the hundreds of

Grotteskew's generally friendly creations: motorized lizard-ladies, skull-faced brains, beetle-bodied bug-boys, steam-powered caterpillars — because wherever he turned, he was reminded of his master's mad genius, and his own insignificance.

But today, Stitch Head didn't have time to hide in the shadows. He raced between the various creations' legs (and wheels and tentacles and robotic parts) as the mad monkey-bat flew from victim to victim, assaulting them.

"AHHH! Oliver, save me!" screamed a two-tailed snake-man with robot arms, as the monkey-bat attacked him from behind. "It's eating my favorite end!"

"Help!" shrieked a tin-plated skeleton. "He wants to kill me! I can feel it in my *bones!*"

"Help! It's going for my phantom limb!" cried a bodiless head.

Even when Stitch Head managed to get close enough to administer a potion, the monkey-bat would simply sneeze and continue his rampage. If he made it to the professor's laboratory, who knew what might happen? Stitch Head had to do something.

He needed help.

"But I was JUST about to take my BATH..." groaned the Creature, as Stitch Head dragged it along the stone corridor towards the commotion-causing monkey-bat.

"He's destroying the castle!" cried Stitch Head. "We have to stop this . . . thing before he does something *terrible*."

"So you REALLY made your very own CREATION?" asked the Creature. "Does that mean you're a MAD PROFESSOR now?"

"No . . . no, of course not!" Stitch Head replied. "I was just . . . trying something. But this thing is, well, he's *mad*."

"But NO ONE is better than YOU at making MAD things UN-MAD," said the Creature. "I mean, you CURED me of werewolfism TWICE! You're the BEST . . ."

"Not this time," Stitch Head replied. "I've created an *incurable monster*! I'm afraid I've made a —"

Stitch Head froze as he noticed sunlight streaming in from the open courtyard door. The monkey-bat was outside. If he flew over the castle walls . . . !

Stitch Head and the Creature crept out into the courtyard. At the far end was the Great Door to the outside world. In the center, perched atop a statue of the professor, was the monkey-bat.

"G<sub>rrrr</sub>RROARRR!"

growled the monkey-bat, his eyes darting around for something to attack.

"Wait . . . THAT'S what you're so WORRIED about?" the Creature said, laughing. "THAT tiny little THINGY?"

"He's trying to escape the castle," said Stitch Head. "We can't let that happen."

"Leave it to ME," said the Creature, stomping toward the statue. "The IMPORTANT thing is to show this thingy who's BOSS!"

"Creature, wait!" cried Stitch Head . . . but it was too late. The Creature was already halfway across the courtyard.

"Now LOOK here, little thingy," began the Creature. "I know how HARD it is being brought to ALMOST-LIFE . . . everything seems so STRANGE and almost-new. But that's a PERFECTLY almost-natural feeling. There's nothing to FEAR. You're among BESTEST friends here!"

The monkey-bat stared at the Creature for a moment, his blood-red eyes all but glowing with feral rage.

"Grrrrrrr . . ."

"Uh-oh," began the Creature. "Why is the thingy GROWLING at me?"

"Creature! Look out!" yelled Stitch Head as the monkey-bat swooped. He landed on the Creature's head and began biting and scratching with all his monstrous rage!

"AAHH! Get him OFF me! He's eating my ears!" squealed the Creature.

Creature began to flail wildly as the monkey-bat ripped chunks of hair off its head with his teeth. "Why didn't you WARN me he was so MONSTROUS?" Creature cried.

Stitch Head raced across the courtyard and climbed the Creature's back until he reached its head. There, he came face to face with the monkey-bat.

"Uh . . . A fast ye . . ." Stitch Head said, nervously drawing his broken sword.

"Yabbit!" shrieked the monkey-bat, preparing to pounce. "GRRAAarrr . . . GRRAAHH!"

At that moment, Stitch Head quite clearly heard the CLUNK-A-KRUNK of a key turning in the Great Door.

It was *opening*! But how? No one could open it, except . . .

"Only me!" said a voice, as the Great Door creaked open. "Boy, this door's heavier

than my old grandma when I have to carry her to the bathroom . . ."

"Arabella! No!" cried Stitch Head, but the monkey-bat had already spotted his escape route. As Arabella emerged from behind the door, Stitch Head's first creation took to the air, gliding straight toward her.

"Arabella, look OUT! He's HUNGRY for HAIR!" screamed the Creature, as the monkey-bat crashed into Arabella, sending them both flying across the courtyard.

"Arabella! No! Go, Creature, go!" shouted Stitch Head, hanging onto what was left of the Creature's hair.

The Creature lumbered toward them as Arabella and the monkey-bat rolled across the ground, kicking up clouds of dust. Arabella's pained screams filled the air . . . or was it *laughter?*

"Hahaha! Finally, a mad thing that's actually got some get-up-and-*gouge!*"

Arabella said. She giggled, as the monkey-bat gnawed happily on her arm. "I was beginning to think there wasn't nothing in this castle with even an ounce of backbone. He's great!"

"He — he is?" asked Stitch Head.

"Sit, mad thing, *sit!*" Arabella ordered.

The monkey-bat immediately flew into the air and landed obediently on Arabella's shoulder. It perched there like a parrot, except with more ear chewing.

"He's a little too tame for my liking," Arabella said, "but he'll do. So can I keep him, Stitch Head?"

"Maybe your POTIONS have finally WORKED," mused the Creature. "Maybe he's CURED. . ."

"Maybe," replied Stitch Head.

He leaped to the ground and tentatively held out a hand to the monkey-bat. The monkey-bat snarled — and immediately tried to bite off a finger. "Or maybe not," said Stitch Head.

"I've never had a pet before — not since that dead rabbit I found a couple years ago," said Arabella, stroking the monkey-bat behind his ears.

"I shall call him . . . Pox," Arabella said. "After the town's last plague, of course."

"But . . ." began Stitch Head. Then he shrugged and smiled weakly. Arabella was clearly the only one who could tame the beast — perhaps he could live without a trusty companion.

Besides . . . Pox hadn't exactly made him feel like a pirate, anyway. Would anything make him feel like a real pirate?

"By the way," continued Arabella, "the mailman handed me a letter. He was too chicken to come up to the castle himself, that big baby."

"A LETTER? Ooh, I LOVE getting letters!" bellowed the Creature. "At least, I would if I ever DID."

"But we never get letters," said Stitch Head suspiciously.

Arabella took the letter out of her dress pocket and handed it to Stitch Head. He stared at the envelope. It was creased and crumpled. Upon it was written:

> *To Be Delivered in Complete Confidence and with Utmost Care to:*
>
> Professor Erasmus
> Castle Grotteskew
> Grubbers Nubbin

"It's for the professor," said Stitch Head, a shiver running down his spine. Suddenly, thoughts of piracy on the high seas seemed very unimportant indeed. Stitch Head felt a strange sense of impending dread . . . as if the outside world was banging on the Great Door.

# THE LETTER
### (Stitch Head's special delivery)

> *"You've been boarded by —*
> *you've been robbed by —*
> *a smooth criminal!"*

From
*The Daring Diary of*
*Captain Flashpowder*

Despite the Creature's insistence that he should "TEAR open!" the envelope, Stitch Head decided that his master should be the first to see whatever the letter inside contained.

So Stitch Head, the Creature and Arabella (accompanied by her new pet, Pox the monkey-bat) made their way to the rafters above the mad professor's laboratory. It was Stitch Head's favorite place in the entire castle.

As always, the professor was hard at work assembling an impressively mad creation. He'd laid out a bizarre assortment of components that he was ordering and reordering in a number of horrifying potential combinations.

"Ah-ha-ha! The knee bone connects to the . . . snake head!" cried the professor. "The elbow connects to the . . . bear paw! AHHHHAHAHA!"

"Are you SURE you don't want a quick PEEK?" asked the Creature, as Stitch Head held the letter in his tiny hands. "What if it's IMPORTANT?"

"I read all my grandma's secret letters," said Arabella. "Of course, my grandma can't actually write, so they don't make much sense . . ."

Stitch Head's fingers hovered over the wax seal.

"I can't," he said finally. "It's not for creation eyes. It's for the professor's eyes only."

He held the letter out in front of him . . . and dropped it. It fluttered gently through the air and landed on the laboratory's center table.

"The shin bone's connected to the . . . antlers! The wrist bone's connected to the . . . horse's hoof? Ahahaha!" cackled the professor.

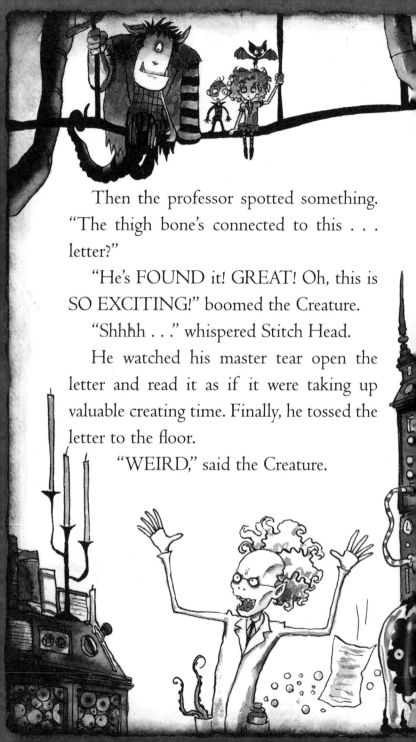

Then the professor spotted something. "The thigh bone's connected to this . . . letter?"

"He's FOUND it! GREAT! Oh, this is SO EXCITING!" boomed the Creature.

"Shhhh . . ." whispered Stitch Head.

He watched his master tear open the letter and read it as if it were taking up valuable creating time. Finally, he tossed the letter to the floor.

"WEIRD," said the Creature.

"Maybe it wasn't so important after all?" Arabella suggested.

"AHAHAHAHAHAHAHAHAAAAA!" screeched the professor. "Finally! After all these long, professoring years! I must pack!"

For the first time in his almost-life, Stitch Head watched the professor abandon his latest creation and leave the laboratory.

"What was that about?" asked Arabella. "He's mad, that mad professor of yours."

"Yabbit!" agreed Pox, spitting out a mouthful of Arabella's hair.

"Forget what I said earlier," said Stitch Head. "We have to read that letter."

After ten minutes of clambering (the Creature suddenly decided it was scared of heights), Stitch Head and his companions made it to the laboratory floor. Stitch Head found the letter in a pile of skulls. He picked it up, took a deep breath, and read it, his heart skipping more beats than usual.

*To the Esteemed Creator of Monsters,*
*Creatures, and Mad Things,*

# CONGRATULATIONS!

Professor Erasmus, YOU have been awarded Mad Professoring's Most Prized Honor, *The Lifetime of Mad Professoring Award!*

The Guild of Mad Professors has chosen you to be our Exceptional Guest at a Most Amazing Ceremony to be held in your honor.

Come to the Grand Olde Town of Oldetown, a day's ride from Castle Grotteskew. We look forward to greeting you at your earliest convenience.

Sincerely,
*PROFESSOR*
*K. E. FARFRIEND,*
*DMP*
(Doctor of Mad Professoring)

"SO, what does it SAY?" asked the Creature.

"He *won*," muttered Stitch Head. "He won a mad professoring award. I didn't even know there was a mad professoring award. But he won. He *won!*"

Stitch Head felt happier than he had in many years. His master's work had finally been recognized! "I always knew — I mean, I always hoped that . . . no one can create like my master! He's the best there is . . ."

"Yeah, it's all very whoop-dee-doo and lah-dee-dah," mocked Arabella, "but don't it mean that the professor is going to —"

# SLAMMMM!

The castle shook with the sound of the Great Door slamming shut.

"He left . . ." whispered Stitch Head.

As it turned out, the professor hadn't even bothered to pack — he'd just left. For the first time in Stitch Head's almost-life, the castle was without its mad professor . . .

. . . And Stitch Head was without a master.

# THE TENTH CHAPTER

# A TRUSTY SHIP

## (Try to focus on the piracy)

*"A pirate without a ship
is like a port without
a starboard!"*

From
*The Daring Diary of
Captain Flashpowder*

Stitch Head had never imagined that the professor would — ever *could* — leave Castle Grotteskew. He'd never even known him to look out the window. He was sure his master would return soon — nothing could keep him away from his work for very long.

But it left Stitch Head feeling strangely lost . . . how should he spend his days if not looking out for his master?

He was still staring at the letter as he and his friends wandered through the dark stone corridors of the castle.

"I know! Let's pretend *we're* MAD PROFESSORS!" boomed the Creature "We can take his PLACE while he's AWAY from the castle!"

"Speaking of which," began Arabella, pointing to Pox as he flew alongside her. "The Creature told me you are Pox's maker. Since when did you start creating creations?"

Stitch Head lowered his head, suddenly embarrassed. "I wasn't professoring," he replied, folding the professor's letter and tucking it into his sleeve. "I was . . . I was trying to make a trusty companion. I was trying to be like Captain Flashpowder."

"I knew it! Is that what that old bit of wood is on your belt?" Arabella said with a laugh. "You're trying to be a pirate!"

"I was just trying to imagine it," mumbled Stitch Head, more ashamed than ever. "I made a list of piratey things. I just thought, because of the eye, maybe I could . . . I don't know. It's *stupid*."

"What are you TALKING about? That's a GREAT idea!" shrieked the Creature with glee. "We can finally pretend we're PIRATES! No more tea parties for us!"

"Sounds good to me," said Arabella. "I ain't done no piracy since Traveling Aunt Olga took me on that cruise . . ."

"I don't know . . . I'm not sure I'm cut out for it," said Stitch Head. "No matter what I do I can't imagine anything except these walls. I just can't see myself as a pirate."

"You just need to think BIGGER!" bellowed the Creature happily. "So, what ELSE is on that LIST of yours?"

Stitch Head didn't get very far down his list. No sooner had he mentioned "a trusty ship" than the Creature squealed with excitement, and jumped up and down with such enthusiasm that the ground beneath their feet began to shake.

"A SHIP! That's PERFECT! We'll BUILD our own PIRATE SHIP! Nothing says 'Look at how PIRATEY I am!' like a nice, big SHIP."

"But how?" asked Stitch Head. "We'd need materials — timber, iron, cloth for the sails . . ."

"You ain't *never* going to discover your inner pirate if you don't start thinking positive," huffed Arabella. "That professor of yours is away for a day or two at least, so we've got the run of the place — an entire castle to plunder! He won't notice

that a few things have gone missing — he
never goes nowhere except that lab of his,
anyway."

"I . . ." began Stitch Head. He didn't
like the idea of stealing from the castle,
despite the fact he'd been stealing from the
professor for years to make his cures.

Then again, building a ship would be
a nice distraction while the professor was
away . . . and Stitch Head really *did* want to
discover his inner pirate. He took a deep
breath.

"Let's do it," he said.

# THE ELEVENTH CHAPTER

# SHIP SHAPE
## (Building the Gadabout II)

*"The trouble with eyepatches
is no one knows
whether you're blinking
or winking."*

From
*The Daring Diary of
Captain Flashpowder*

Arabella was quick to come up with a strategy for building Stitch Head's pirate ship.

They would work in the courtyard so they would have plenty of space for all the masts, jibs, bowsprits, and topsails.

Stitch Head would design it, based on the drawings of the *Gadabout* in *The Daring Diary of Captain Flashpowder.*

The Creature would use its strength, ingenuity, and friends within the creation community to gather the materials they needed (the Creature ran both the Arts 'n' Crafts Club and the Creative Creations Collective Class).

Then Arabella would direct the building process by shouting very loudly at everyone.

"Faster, you lax 'n' lazy landlubbers! Pick up them feet or I'll make you walk the plank! And I'll make sure the waters are shark infested!" she screamed, holding Pox by the tail as he gnashed and growled.

"YES, sir! I mean, MA'AM! Err, I mean . . ." replied the Creature, stomping past with a handful of wooden doors it had borrowed from various rooms around the castle.

Arabella giggled. "This is fun!" she said.

A moment later, Stitch Head emerged with a large, carefully rolled-up piece of paper — his design for their ship.

"I finished!" Stitch Head said. "What do you —"

"Speak up, you butt-brain!" yelled Arabella, snatching the design. "I don't want no mumbling unless I give you a direct mumbling order!" She unrolled the paper. "I should have you swab the deck with this — hey, this is really good!"

Arabella laid the design on the ground. It was a remarkably accurate copy of the *Gadabout.* In fact, Stitch Head had named his ship the *Gadabout II.* A dark, imposing sail hung from the ship's mast. In its center was the pirates' symbol, the skull and crossbones, but with one notable difference — the skull was outlined with *stitches.*

"This is going to be a fine ship, Stitch Head," said Arabella with a smile. "I reckon you might have found your inner pirate after all!"

Stitch Head, Arabella, and the Creature worked for a day and a night on the ship, stopping only for naps and food. The Creature was a particular fan of both, even though it didn't need either.

Stitch Head, however, never stopped. He sawed, hammered, bolted, and sewed as if his almost-life depended on it, all the while hoping that it would trigger something in his imagination — that it would reveal his inner pirate.

By the morning of the second day, the *Gadabout II* was complete. It was fair to say it didn't look exactly like Stitch Head's design. In fact, it didn't look anything like it at all.

But that fact didn't seem to bother the Creature. "It's GREAT! The BESTEST pirate ship EVER!" he hollered.

Stitch Head glanced at the ship. It was a lot smaller than he'd hoped — only slightly bigger than the Creature — and its hull was cobbled together with random pieces of wood that were clumsily nailed or tied together.

The sails were even more shabby — far from being vast, dark, and imposing, they were a messy patchwork of floral-patterned bedsheets.

"Nah, it's a real mess!" chuckled Arabella. "But it's a ship — your ship, Stitch Head. Why don't you try it out?"

Stitch Head climbed aboard. The ship creaked and rattled as if it might fall to pieces at any moment. He cautiously inched toward the bow, drew his sword, and struck his most pirate-like pose. He tried to imagine the vast, blue oceans, the cool sea breeze, the distant islands . . .

"Onward . . . to adventure," Stitch Head whispered, but to his disappointment, he didn't *feel* any different. He still felt like a forgotten creation standing on a ramshackle boat.

Stitch Head sighed. Perhaps it was for the best — if he could never leave the castle, why bother trying to pretend he was anything other than a forgotten creation?

"SO? Have you found your INNER pirate?" asked the Creature, clapping two of its three hands together in excitement.

Stitch Head looked down at the expectant faces of his friends. He hated to lie, but they had worked so hard, he couldn't bear to tell them the truth. Finally, he said, "I think I have. I feel like Captain Flashpowder. Thank you . . . for everything. I guess I am part pirate after all."

"I KNEW it!" boomed the Creature.

"Sounds like a job well done!" said Arabella. "Well, I'd best be heading back to Grubbers Nubbin. I ain't eaten nothing but sawdust and beetles all day — I'm starving."

Arabella rubbed Pox on the belly and made him promise not to attack anyone until her next visit. He gave a reluctant "GRuKK!" and then bit her on the ankle.

"Next time I come over, we're taking that thing down to Grubbers Harbor and setting sail," said Arabella. She unlocked the Great Door, heaved it open, and made her way outside. "See you tomorrow. Hang on, what's this?" She reappeared with something in her hand.

It was another letter.

# THE SECOND LETTER

## (Dear Stitch Head)

*"Never trust a message in a bottle.
Unless it's a treasure map!"*

From
*The Daring Diary of
Captain Flashpowder*

Stitch Head jumped down from the *Gadabout II* and took the letter. His jaw dropped as he stared at the front of the envelope.

To:
Stitch Head
Castle Grotteskew
Grubbers Nubbin

"For . . . me?" he whispered in horror. "But no one knows I even — I mean, no one knows I *exist*. Except . . ."

"OPEN IT!" screamed the Creature. "Is it a LOVE letter? A GOLDEN ticket to a land of CHOCOLATE? The SUSPENSE is KILLING me!"

Stitch Head tore open the letter.

Dear Stitch Head (and other monsters, creatures, and mad things of Castle Grotteskew),

I write to tell you that I have discovered a most genuine life of fame, fortune, and fulfillment in the Outside World. In truth, everyone here considers me a genius, and proclaims that my mad professoring is the finest (and maddest) of all.

I am famous!

And so, I must tell you that I am abandoning my life in the castle. I shall not return to Grotteskew, ever, ever again. Ever!

Farewell, creations of Grotteskew! Long may the castle loom above Grubbers Nubbin . . . or crumble to the ground. What do I care? I have forgotten all of you already!

Sincerely,
Mad Professor Erasmus

Stitch Head stared at the words, unable to breathe.

"What does it SAY? Have you won a PRIZE?" boomed the Creature. "I *LOVE* winning prizes! I expect —"

"Stitch Head, what is it?" asked Arabella, her voice suddenly soft. "What does it say?"

"He's gone," replied Stitch Head. "My master's not coming back."

Stitch Head slumped to his knees. He tried to read the letter again, but tears welled up in his eyes and blurred his vision.

Under any other circumstances, Stitch Head would have been delighted that the professor had chosen to write to him, of all the creations in the castle. But to abandon the castle . . . to abandon his work . . . to abandon *him* . . . Stitch Head felt anger and sadness bubbling up inside him.

"I don't UNDERSTAND," said the Creature finally. "What does the OUTSIDE world have that the CASTLE doesn't? Apart from FRESH AIR, proper PLUMBING, and actual HUMAN beings . . ."

"Forget the professor, Stitch Head — you don't need that crusty old castle-crasher!" said Arabella, trying to cheer him

up. "You've got your whole almost-life ahead of you! You don't want to spend it cleaning up after someone who hardly even knows you exist . . . right?"

But in truth, that was exactly what Stitch Head wanted. He wiped away his tears and got to his feet. "I'm sorry . . . I have to go."

"Go WHERE?" asked the Creature.

"I don't know," replied Stitch Head. He hurried out of the courtyard and disappeared into the enveloping gloom of the castle.

# THE THIRTEENTH CHAPTER

# MOAT FLOAT
## (Cheering up Stitch Head)

*"When you're at the bottom
of the ocean, the only way
is up."*

From
*The Daring Diary of
Captain Flashpowder*

Stitch Head wandered through the castle, feeling more lost and lonely than he had for years. He had no idea where he was going, or what he was going to do now that he was a creation without a master.

What's worse, he felt as if he was seeing Grotteskew for the first time. The crumbling, stone walls. The bleak, unlit corridors. The vast, hollow chambers. It all seemed cold and unwelcoming.

He thought about returning to the dungeons of Grotteskew, far from the other creations, hoping that he might feel like he belonged there. Or at least perhaps the darkness might swallow him up.

But instead, he found himself in the Forgotten Room, sitting amongst the toys and books and dust.

Perhaps the professor had been right to leave him there. Perhaps he never should have left. Perhaps this was where Stitch Head belonged.

He didn't know how long he had been sitting there. Minutes? Maybe hours? But then he heard a familiar sound.

"Yabbit!"

Stitch Head spun around to see Arabella standing in the doorway. Pox was perched on her shoulder, grumbling loudly.

"Thought I might find you here," said Arabella. "Ain't no good sitting around *moping*."

"Please," said Stitch Head, bowing his head. "I . . . just leave me alone. I want to be alone."

"Not a chance," replied Arabella, sitting down next to him. "My grandma always says the only thing worse than moping is getting your head kicked in by a horse — and she's done both in her time. You need someone to cheer you up, whether you like it or not."

"I really don't feel like —" began Stitch Head, but Arabella wasn't finished.

"The fact is, the professor's gone. Now you can sit here and wait for him to come back, just like you sat here all them years . . . but he ain't coming back, and you know it. You're free! And you're part pirate! There's a whole world out there — adventure and treasure and all sorts of stuff — all there for the taking!"

"I can't," replied Stitch Head. "I *promised*."

"Promised what? You can't protect him if he ain't here! I told you once and I'll tell you again — you gotta get out more."

"I can't!" repeated Stitch Head. "Last time I opened those gates the castle nearly

fell! I trusted Fulbert Freakfinder because I wanted to be something I'm not . . . I'm a forgotten creation and that's all I'll ever —"

"No moping, I said!" snapped Arabella. She grabbed Stitch Head and pulled him toward the window. "I've got a surprise for you. See down there? In the moat?"

Stitch Head peered into the gloom of the dusk. He could see the glistening waters of the castle moat that surrounded Grotteskew. And on the bank . . .

"Is . . . is that the Creature?" whispered Stitch Head.

"It sure is! I gave it my key! First time beyond the castle walls, and loving it!" said Arabella, poking her head out of the window. "Hey, Creature!"

The Creature looked up at the window and gave a happy wave. Arabella gave it the thumbs up. It disappeared behind a large tree.

"Where's it going?" asked Stitch Head. After a moment, the Creature reappeared . . . dragging the *Gadabout II* along the ground behind it.

"Time you see what you're missing," said Arabella. "We're going to show you the life you could have. A life beyond these walls — a *pirate's* life."

Stitch Head watched in amazement as the Creature dragged the ship to the edge of the moat. Then, with an almighty shove, it pushed it into the water with a thunderous SPLOSH!

"A trusty ship!" said Arabella, as the *Gadabout II* bobbed about on the water. Despite its shape and haphazard strangeness, it looked rather majestic. Perfect, perhaps, for a strange, haphazard pirate.

It was then the water began to bubble, and the ship bobbed awkwardly. A moment later, it started to sink.

"OH, NO!" screamed the Creature.

The Creature jumped in after the ship, without realizing it couldn't swim. It flailed around a bit before scrambling desperately back to the shore, just in time to see the *Gadabout II* vanish beneath the water.

"*Huh,*" grunted Arabella, as she watched the bow of the ship disappear into the moat. She turned to Stitch Head. "Any chance you didn't see that last part?"

"Thank you for trying to cheer me up. I appreciate it, I really do," whispered Stitch Head. He looked around the Forgotten Room. "But I'm no pirate, eye or no eye. This is my almost-life, here, in the castle. *This* is all I've ever known. It's . . . it's all I can imagine."

Arabella sighed. "I have to go home," she said. "But I'll be back soon, all right? And if you need anything, you know where I'll be."

"Thank you," Stitch Head replied. He watched Arabella leave, and then sat back down among the toys and the books and the dust.

# THE PIRATE'S EYE

## (The Creature gives Stitch Head a present)

*"You've never seen the world until you've seen it through an eyepatch."*

From
*The Daring Diary of Captain Flashpowder*

Stitch Head had been sitting in the Forgotten Room for a few hours, watching the sun set outside the window. At the very moment dusk was about to fall, a crumpled envelope dropped from above and landed next to him. He felt his heart skip. *Another letter?* he thought. *Could it be from the professor?*

He looked up and saw a conspicuous shape peering over the hole in the ceiling. The shape disappeared into the shadows with a giggle, and Stitch Head realized immediately that it was the Creature. What was it up to? Was it some sort of game? He picked up the envelope and opened it, finding a note inside.

DEAR STICH HEAD
SORRY ABOWT SINKING
YOUR PIRATE SHIP!
ARABELA SAYED YOU
WONTED TO BE ALONE.

BUT I THOT YOU MIGHT LIKE A PRESENT.
(IT'S SOMETHING YOU DIDN'T PUT ON YOR LIST.
I HOPE IT HELLPS!

YOR BESTEST FREND,
THE CREATURE

Stitch Head looked inside the envelope. There was a long strip of black cloth, thin at each end but wide in the middle. He took it out and inspected it. At first he had no idea what it could be, but then it struck him.

It was an *eyepatch.*

Stitch Head shook his head. It was far too late for eyepatches, pirates, and adventures.

Nevertheless, Stitch Head was grateful that the Creature had tried to help — and felt kind of guilty that it had made the effort. He smiled faintly, and then found himself covering his left eye with the eyepatch and tying it around his head. For the first time, he saw the world only out of his ice-blue eye.

Slowly, the gloom of the castle seemed to fade. The light of dusk was replaced with a bright, white light that seemed to burst through every crack and crevice. The dark, stone walls appeared to melt, and in their place stretched the endless, glimmering ocean. Stitch Head looked up to see the ceiling vanish and reveal the bright, morning sky. It was as if the Forgotten Room had disappeared. In his mind, Stitch Head saw the white crests of the crashing waves, the spiraling light of the afternoon sun, the seagulls soaring above him and singing his name. He felt the warm ocean spray on his face as his grand pirate ship rose and crashed through the water, sailing proudly toward an island filled with untold riches — and *adventure*.

"I can see it! I can see it all," whispered Stitch Head. In that moment, he felt more free than he ever had . . . and he knew he was a pirate.

Stitch Head raced through the castle, his patch over his eye and his sword by his side.

"Creature! Creature! I'm part pirate, I can see it now!" he cried, as he hurried down corridor after corridor. He finally found the Creature in a large chamber in the south wing playing a card game with a tin-plated turkey and a wheel-footed wolf-woman.

"The eyepatch — it worked!" cried Stitch Head. "All I had to do was look at things through Flashpowder's eye!"

"GREAT!" said the Creature, not entirely sure what that meant. "I'm SO glad we can FINALLY play PIRATES now!"

"What's the point of playing? What's the point of me staying here at all if the professor has gone forever? And if he's not here to make any more creations, I don't have to worry about making any more cures!" replied Stitch Head. He suddenly noticed the other creations in the room. For the first time in his almost-life, he didn't feel the slightest need to stay hidden.

"Sorry to interrupt," Stitch Head said with a smile.

"Interrupt away, my young friend," replied the wolf-woman. "I have the world's worst hand of cards, anyway."

"Creature, I'm ready!" continued Stitch Head. "I'm ready to sail the seven seas! I'm ready for adventure! We just need to get my ship!"

"Um . . . I THINK I may have probably DEFINITELY sunk the ship," said the Creature.

"Don't worry," replied Stitch Head. "I have an idea!"

# THE FIFTEENTH CHAPTER

# RAISING THE GADABOUT II
## (Just whistle)

*"You can never have too much gold! Unless it makes your ship sink."*

From
*The Daring Diary of Captain Flashpowder*

For the second time in his almost-life, Stitch Head opened the Great Door and stepped out into the night air. But this time, there was no Fulbert Freakfinder waiting for him on the other side. Stitch Head saw a world of possibilities and adventure. That was the world through a pirate's eye — the world that Captain Flashpowder must have seen.

Stitch Head adjusted his eyepatch, and then he and the Creature hurried down to the bank of the moat.

"Time to call in a favor," said Stitch Head. He put two fingers in his mouth and whistled.

## "Ffffpfpfpf!"

It wasn't so much of a whistle as a strange, wet growl — like a cat farting.

"Sorry," Stitch Head muttered. "I've never tried to whistle before."

"Wait, are you WHISTLING? I LOVE whistling!" boomed the Creature. "The OTHER creations won't let me DO it because it makes their TEETH fall out . . . the ones that HAVE teeth, that is."

The Creature put two fingers from each of its three hands into its mouth — and blew!

The sound made Stitch Head's stitches ache. He covered his ears as the whistle rang out through the air.

"That should do it!" Stitch Head whimpered. He peered into the moat. After a moment, the water began to bubble and churn. Then something slowly started to emerge.

"The *Gadabout II!*" cried the Creature, as the ship slowly rose from the depths. "Am I DOING this? Do I have a MAGIC whistle?"

"I don't think so . . ." whispered Stitch Head.

A moment later, the *Gadabout II* was back on the surface of the water, leaking from numerous gaps in the hull. But it didn't stop rising until it was completely clear of the water. Wrapped around the base of the hull were eight tentacles.

"It's him!" whispered Stitch Head, a smile spreading across his face.

"*Him?* Him WHO?" the Creature asked.

"*Him!* I mean *it!* I mean the octo-monster!" Stitch Head stammered.

"A good evening to you, my fellow creations!" said the octo-monster as it hoisted the *Gadabout II* out of the water and onto the bank. "I assume you've come to collect your sunken vessel."

"Thank you, um . . ." began Stitch Head. "What's your name?"

"Call me *Updike!*" the octo-monster said, bowing as much as an octopus can bow. "And it's the very least I can do to thank you for bringing me to my senses. Enjoy your ship! Although . . . I feel honor-bound to point out there are one or two fairly large holes in the hull. Did you not intend it to float?"

"It's . . . a work in progress," replied Stitch Head, plugging a hole in the ship's hull with his finger. "But it *will* float, I promise. Thanks, Updike."

Stitch Head and the Creature spent the next few hours getting the *Gadabout II* shipshape and leak proof. After another, more successful maiden voyage in the moat, Stitch Head was ready to set sail.

Almost.

"It's so *far*," whispered Stitch Head, staring out across the moonlit landscape. "The ocean seemed much closer from up in the castle. I've barely been outside the Great Door and now look at me! I'm trying to sail a ship to the ocean!"

"Don't WORRY, I have everything under CONTROL," said the Creature. It grabbed the *Gadabout II* in its two strongest arms. With one powerful heave, it hoisted the ship onto its back.

"HurRrG!" grunted the Creature. "To the OCEAN! Via ADVENTURE! And Grubbers Nubbin."

"Creature . . . you'd do that for me?" Stitch Head asked. "You'd leave Grotteskew? And carry the ship all the way to the sea?"

"Well, you're NOT going to be much of a PIRATE without a CRUSTY crew, now, ARE you?" replied the Creature.

"A *crusty* crew . . . ?" replied Stitch Head. "You mean a *trusty* —"

"I MEAN I want to be a PIRATE, too! I'm SICK of tea parties! I want to go on a GREAT ADVENTURE with my BESTEST friend. What do you SAY?"

"I say . . . *yes!*" said Stitch Head.

"GREAT! We were HOPING you'd agree!" boomed the Creature gleefully. It put two fingers from its unoccupied third hand into its mouth.

"ThweeeEEEP!"

A moment later, Pox swooped down from his perch atop the castle's parapets, yapping and growling. He landed on the ground next to Stitch Head and hissed angrily in his face.

"Uh, Creature?" Stitch Head whispered. "I don't think I need Pox as a trusty companion . . ."

"It's not FOR you," replied the Creature. "Arabella said she'd ONLY come with us if we BROUGHT him along."

# THE SIXTEENTH CHAPTER

# A TRUSTY CREW

## (Let's get this show on the sea!)

*"There's no crew like
a trusty crew."*

From
*The Daring Diary of
Captain Flashpowder*

Under the cover of darkness, Stitch Head, the Creature (still carrying the *Gadabout II* upon its back), and their not-so-trusty companion, Pox, made the slow trek to Grubbers Nubbin to collect the last member of the crew.

Stitch Head had always been frightened of the land beyond the castle. It was so wide open — it seemed there was nowhere to hide. But tonight, through his pirate's eye, the world without walls looked like an adventure waiting to happen.

They crept towards the outskirts of Grubbers Nubbin, a few dim lamplights still burning in the sleeping town.

"I hope no one SPOTS us," said the Creature. "I don't want to SCARE anyone. Last time I saw my reflection in the water, I SCREAMED for nearly an HOUR."

"Ha! I've had scarier knee scabs," said Arabella, stepping out from behind a tree.

"Swartiki!" yapped Pox happily. He flew toward Arabella, landed on her head, and immediately started chewing her hair.

"Arabella! How did you know we were coming?" asked Stitch Head.

Arabella shook her head. "The Creature carrying a ship on its back. I saw that coming from a mile away. I've been looking for you . . . I knew you'd eventually come around. So let's get this show on the road! I mean, sea."

"Arabella, are — are you sure about this?" asked Stitch Head. "I don't know how long we'll be gone. Your life here . . . what about your grandma?"

"My grandma? She don't even know what *day* it is. She don't know who I am half the time," said Arabella with a shrug. "Anyway, I haven't had a *real* adventure in months! So if you're planning on setting sail, you'd better make room for me and my new pirating boots."

Stitch Head smiled broadly. "Welcome aboard," he said.

# THE SEVENTEENTH CHAPTER

# GRUBBERS HARBOR

## (The voice on the wind)

*"Sail away, sail away,
sail away!"*

From
*The Daring Diary of
Captain Flashpowder*

With his trusty crew complete, Stitch Head felt more ready than ever for a pirate's life. They snuck through the cobbled streets of Grubbers Nubbin and followed the winding road down to the sea. Dawn was beginning to break over the horizon when Stitch Head finally smelled the sharp, salty air of the ocean.

They had arrived at Grubbers Harbor!

The sea was even more magnificent than it had been in Stitch Head's imagination. It stretched endlessly into the distance — a great, gleaming ocean of possibilities. Who knew what kinds of adventures were waiting for him out there?

"Okay, men!" Arabella cried. "Let's get this party started!"

In the near distance was a circular bay filled with dozens of boats and ships. At the far end of the harbor were several hefty sailors were loading a large ship with cargo.

Stitch Head and his trusty crew were careful not to be seen as they hurried down to the bay, then scurried along a wooden dock that jutted out into the sea. As soon as they reached the end of the dock, the Creature hefted the *Gadabout II* off its shoulders and deposited it in the water.

"It floats!" the Creature cried happily. They all watched the ship bob in the water.

"Don't just stand there, landlubbers!" said Arabella.

She jumped into the ship. The Creature followed, taking up almost the entire deck. For a moment, Stitch Head paused.

"Hoist the middle mast!" he finally cried, leaping aboard. He grabbed the ship's wheel and did his best to steer it straight as the tide carried them out to sea.

"We did it," cried Stitch Head, looking back. In the far distance he could just make out the distant spires of Castle Grotteskew. "Onward . . . to *adventure*."

He used his pirate's eye to glance out at the sea, and felt the chilly air whistle past his ears. It sounded like a voice, as if the ocean itself was whisper secrets to him.

"Unhand me, you fiends!" the wind seemed to cry out. Oddly, Stitch Head though the ocean breeze sounded a lot like his master.

"I said, unhand me! I'm too important to be manhandled!" the wind whispered again.

"Master . . . ?" Stitch Head whispered, certain he heard the professor's voice.

"Are you okay, Stitch Head?" asked the Creature, trying to find a place to sit on the tiny ship.

Stitch Head peered across the bay at a large ship on the horizon. On the ship's ramp, two men were arguing. He could only see one of them clearly — he was a tall, broad-shouldered man with a thick, black beard. The other man was short and fat with skinny legs. He was dragging a large sack that writhed and squirmed.

As the *Gadabout II* bobbed out of the bay, Stitch Head strained to hear what the men were saying.

"Listen to me!" the fat man said. "It took me forever to book a ship that would take *any* cargo! No questions asked, you said!"

"A human being is not cargo!" the skinny man said. "I be the cap'n of this ship! It be my neck on the line if we're caught."

"It's more money you're after, is it?" the fat man said. "Lugs and mumbles, you drive a hard bargain, cap'n!"

Stitch Head watched as the fat man handed the skinny cap'n a wad of money.

The cap'n nodded, and the fat man began lifting the sack onto the edge of one of the empty crates. As the man turned, Stitch Head finally got a look at his face. His eye grew wide. Including the professor, Stitch Head had only met three human people in his almost-life . . . and the fat man was one of them.

"Fulbert Freakfinder . . . !" Stitch Head whispered, his mouth agape.

Stitch Head watched as Freakfinder emptied out the sack. A bony, silver-haired old man fell out and tumbled into the crate.

"Oooof! You can't treat me like this! I'm an award-winning mad professor!" the silver-haired man said.

It was Professor Erasmus!

# FOLLOW THAT SHIP
## (Stitch Head sets sail)

*"The journey to adventure
is paved with ocean."*

From
*The Daring Diary of
Captain Flashpowder*

Stitch Head stared in horror as Fulbert Freakfinder locked the professor inside the crate.

"Th-that ship … Master … Freakfinder!" Stitch Head stuttered.

"Are you okay, Stitch Head?" asked the Creature, rocking the *Gadabout II* as it struggled to get comfy.

"Yeah, what are you rambling about? You ain't making any sense," said Arabella.

"Fulbert Freakfinder has kidnapped the professor, and he's on *that* ship!" cried Stitch Head, snapping out of his daze.

They watched the ship raise anchor and begin to pull out of the harbor. Stitch Head grabbed their ship's wheel and turned it frantically. "We have to save him! Hoist the sail, quickly!"

"FULBERT FREAKFINDER? Are you SURE?" asked the Creature. "As in *THE* Fulbert Freakfinder, your ARCH-ENEMY!"

"Yes, it's Fulbert Freakfinder, I'm sure of it!" yelled Stitch Head, carefully steering the *Gadabout II* toward the horizon. "Follow that ship!"

"I give the orders around here. . ." said Arabella, releasing the mainsail's bindings. The ragged, patchwork sail unfurled and caught a strong current of air. With a great WHOMPH, the *Gadabout II* lurched and bobbed as they were ushered out to sea.

"Hang on! The wind is at our backs now!" cried Arabella.

The *Gadabout II* sped across the waves, rattling and creaking.

The ship sounded like it was about to come apart. Stitch Head hung on for dear almost-life, his pirate's eye fixed on the other ship.

"What's FREAKFINDER doing on a SHIP with the PROFESSOR?" shouted the Creature.

"I don't know . . . but I know what he wants with him," said Stitch Head grimly. "Freakfinder needs crazy things for his Traveling Carnival of Unnatural Wonders. He's going to force the professor to create more freaks for his shows."

"That pig-faced plotter!" snapped Arabella. "How did he get his hairy hands on the prof?"

"The award! Freakfinder must have been watching the castle . . . or he knew the professor was leaving — but how? Memories flashed through Stitch Head's mind like lightning. He took the two letters out of his sleeve and unfolded them. His eye darted to the bottom of the first letter.

*Professor K. E. Farfriend, DMP* (Doctor of Mad Professoring).

"K. E. Farfriend . . ." Stitch Head muttered. Slowly, the letters began to un-jumble in his mind.

K F
A
I
N E
I F
D E
R R

"FREAKFINDER!" bellowed the Creature. Stitch Head and Arabella stared at him in disbelief. "I play a LOT of SCRABBLE," the Creature added proudly.

"Oh, no . . . I've been such an idiot," said Stitch Head, holding both letters next to each other. "I couldn't see what was right in front of my pirate eye . . . these letters are from *Fulbert Freakfinder*."

"Swar-tikki?" yapped Pox.

"Yeah, what are you talking about?" asked Arabella.

"It's a trick . . . it's all a big trick!" cried Stitch Head. He held up the letters. "Freakfinder wrote the first letter to lure the professor out of the castle so he could kidnap him! Then he sent the second letter from the professor to me — to stop us from going after him. They're even in the same handwriting — look!"

"THAT means . . ." began the Creature.

"It means we have to save the professor!" cried Stitch Head.

"That big ol' ship is getting away twice as fast as we're moving," said Arabella. "We ain't never going to catch it at this rate."

Sure enough, the other ship, with its many impressive-looking sails, was speeding away across the water.

"We have to go faster!" cried Stitch Head.

"We can't!" said Arabella. "This is as fast as we go unless we lose some weight!"

"We don't have anything to lose!" said Stitch Head. "There's no room for anything on this ship but us!" For a moment he thought he could hear the professor's cries, but it was just the sound of the wind.

"Lose WEIGHT, huh?" said the Creature. It put one of its three hands on Stitch Head's shoulder. "Rescue your master. I KNOW you can do it. I BELIEVE in you. Remember . . . you're a *real* PIRATE now."

The Creature jumped to its feet, pinched its nose with its third hand . . . and threw itself overboard.

## SPLOOOOooooSH!

"Creature! No!" cried Stitch Head.

"What are BESTEST friends for?" cried the Creature, gurgling as it tried to stay afloat.

"We can't leave you! You can't even swim!" said Stitch Head.

"All the more REASON to practice my DOGGY-paddle," replied the Creature, frantically thrashing all three of its arms. "Now GO!"

Stitch Head had little choice. Without the Creature, the *Gadabout II* was half as heavy — a decent gust of wind was all it took to send it speeding across the water. Within moments, they were gaining on the other ship . . . and the Creature was just a speck in the ocean.

# THE NINETEENTH CHAPTER

# ALL ABOARD
## (Hijinks on the high seas)

*"I've never met a ship
I didn't want to board."*

From
*The Daring Diary of
Captain Flashpowder*

Stitch Head held on as the *Gadabout II* sped through the waves.

"Creature . . ." said Stitch Head. "Do — do you think it's going to be okay?"

"No point in crying about it now — we're gaining on the ship!" said Arabella. "Get your head back in the game! You're a *pirate* now."

"I'm a pirate now," Stitch Head repeated, turning back to face the horizon.

He steered the ship and felt the wind on the back of his head driving them on. The *Gadabout II* bounced and careened along the surface of the water like a skipping stone. With the extra speed they'd gained by losing the Creature, they were quickly catching up with the other ship — and the professor. Before long, they were neck and neck.

"It's now or never!" cried Stitch Head. "Arabella, grab the wheel! Bring us in as close as you can!"

Arabella grabbed the ship's wheel and turned it to the left. The *Gadabout II* bobbed nearer to the hull of the other ship, getting closer and closer, until Stitch Head feared the two ships might crash together.

"Now what?" said Arabella, trying to hold the ship steady.

"What would Captain Flashpowder do?" Stitch Head muttered to himself. He aimed his pirate's eye down at the broken sword tucked into his belt.

A moment later, an idea came to him like a flash of light. He quickly untied the sail rope and rolled it up. Then he drew his sword and tied it to one end of the sturdy rope.

"GLurK!" barked Pox.

"Whatever you're going to do — do it *now!*" cried Arabella.

Stitch Head started swinging the rope around his head faster and faster, until it filled the humid air with a shrill whistling sound.

Stitch Head narrowed his eyes . . . then he threw the sword as hard as he could! The broken sword flew through the air, clanking onto the deck of the other ship. Stitch Head yanked the rope and felt the sword catch hold on the deck's edge.

"As soon as you let go of the wheel, grab onto me!" cried Stitch Head, gripping the rope tightly. He peered over the edge of their boat into the churning water. He adjusted his eyepatch. "We have to swing for it! Prepare for boarding!"

"*Now* you're talking!" said Arabella. She let go of the ship's wheel and grabbed hold of Stitch Head's tiny shoulders as the *Gadabout II* began to veer away.

Stitch Head closed his pirate eye — and leaped from the ship! They swung away, then crashed into the hull of the other ship.

Stitch Head hung on for dear almost-life, his stitches ready to burst as Arabella locked her elbows around his neck. He quickly realized he wasn't strong enough to carry them up the rope.

"Yabbit!" growled Pox, as he flapped around them. Stitch Head opened his eye to see Arabella grasp the rope above his head and climb over him. She shimmied to the top and scrambled over the side of the ship and onto the deck. Then she leaned back over and held out her free hand.

"We ain't got all day — grab hold!" Arabella whispered.

Stitch Head reached up and grasped Arabella's hand. She pulled with all her might, hauling him onto the deck.

"Thanks!" whispered Stitch Head, untying his sword from the rope.

"Nice swinging — you're really getting the *hang* of this pirate stuff," she replied with a laugh. Pox landed on her shoulder.

The ship was huge. Stitch Head led Arabella behind a large barrel on the side of the deck. He peered out from behind it and looked around.

They were halfway between the bow at the front of the ship, and the stern. The rear of the wooden deck was piled high with crates, caskets, and barrels, while the bow was filled with a dozen burly-looking crewmen. Above them, a spiderweb of rigging stretched high above the billowing sails.

"So, what now?" Arabella asked.

Stitch Head's ice-blue eye glinted in the brightening sunlight.

"Now we find the professor," he said in his most piratey voice.

# THE TWENTIETH CHAPTER

# CRATE EXPECTATIONS
## (Finding the professor)

"*A true pirate always keeps his buckles swashed.*"

From
*The Daring Diary of
Captain Flashpowder*

"Pox, fly up to the rigging and stay out of sight," said Stitch Head, as they huddled behind the barrel. "Wait there and watch for my signal."

Pox stared at Stitch Head and then snarled angrily at him.

"Uh, please?" he asked nervously.

"Do what he says, you grump, or no hair chewing for a week," said Arabella. Pox grunted and then flew up into the sails.

"I say we go in, all boots kicking," said Arabella, tightening her laces. "I'm in the mood to kick some —"

"Let me out right now!" cried a voice. "I'll miss the award ceremony!"

"The professor!" whispered Stitch Head.

"Arabella — he's in one of those crates! Follow me . . . and *please* don't pick a fight with anyone just yet."

Arabella gave an annoyed nod and followed Stitch Head. They crept silently along the edge of the deck toward the crates, ducking between barrels and lifeboats. Stitch Head craned his neck to listen over the sound of the whistling wind.

"Release me, right this moment! I'm getting a cramp in my professoring hand!"

"This way . . . no, that way," said Stitch
Head, moving along the huge stack of
crates. He scurried up onto one, then
another.

"You'll regret this! I'm quite famous
for my madness!"

"Does he ever shut up?" asked Arabella
as she kept a lookout from the deck.

At the top of the pile sat a crate that
rattled and shook. "Un-box me this instant!
I must return to my laboratory!"

"Professor, it's all right, we are here!"
said Stitch Head, reaching the crate. It's
Stitch Head! We're here to rescue you!"

The crate stopped rattling.

"Who?" asked the professor.

"Stitch Head . . . your first creation.
We've traveled the several seas to rescue
you!"

"Stitch Head . . . Stitch Head . . . the
name sort of rings a bell . . ." mumbled the
professor.

Stitch Head sighed. He suddenly felt smaller than ever for imagining that his master would remember him . . . but then *he* remembered something.

Only he had the pirate's eye.

"Sit tight, my master, we're going to get you out of that big crate!" Stitch Head said. "Then we're going to get you back to Castle Grotteskew, where —"

"Lugs and mumbles, it can't really be . . . *Stitch Head*?" a voice cried from below.

Stitch Head spun around and looked down at the deck. The fat face of Fulbert Freakfinder was staring up at him.

# FIENDISH FULBERT FREAKFINDER

## (What would Captain Flashpowder do?)

*"If in doubt, draw your sword!"*

From
*The Daring Diary of
Captain Flashpowder*

"We've been found! Let's get kicking!" cried Arabella.

Freakfinder gasped. "Impossible!" he said. He pointed his cane at Stitch Head. "How did you work out my most excellent plan? It was foolproof! Why, all that effort I went through to forge that letter from Professor Erasmus . . ."

Stitch Head suddenly felt a burning need to confess the truth — that he had simply stumbled across Freakfinder's fiendish plot. That he had chosen the life of a pirate over his master — but Arabella was quicker to speak her mind.

"Yeah, well, your plan was a load of stinky rubbish, because here we are!" she shouted. "You didn't even bother to change your handwriting, stupid fatty pig-face!"

"I remember you, too, you rude little snot," growled Freakfinder. "But I must admit, I'm impressed . . . leavin' the castle, trackin' me down, smugglin' yourselves aboard the ship. But what's your plan now, Stitch Head? Save your precious master and swim back to shore? HA! Lugs and mumbles, you're such fools!"

"You scheming slug! I'll kick that smug grin off your face!" growled Arabella.

"I believe you might try, little snot . . . but you can't kick us all," said Fulbert Freakfinder. He took a deep breath and yelled, "Intruders! Stowaways! Sound the alarm!"

"Oh, no . . . Arabella! Up here! Climb!" cried Stitch Head.

Arabella climbed up the crates as a dozen crewmen appeared from below the deck, each one bigger than the last. They gathered around the stack of crates, grinding their teeth and cracking their knuckles. On the other side of the crates was the edge of the ship . . . and a long fall to a watery grave.

The tall, bearded man from the harbor stepped through the crowd and peered up at them. "Stowaways, be it?" he said. "And *children*, at that! Well, I be cap'n of this vessel, so what I say goes. Down you get off there. I'm sure your parents are worried sick about you." He peered at Stitch Head. "Especially you — you look like you should be in the hospital!"

"Leave them to me, cap'n," Freakfinder said with a sneer. "I shall ensure that they never bother you again."

"Try it, you pudgy pig!" snapped Arabella.

"Wait, do you know these characters, Freakfinder?" asked the cap'n.

"That I do, cap'n. That patchwork rag doll calls himself Stitch Head, believe it or not," Freakfinder said with a chuckle. "The eyepatch is new, though. You playin' at being a pirate now, Stitch Head?"

"I . . . I'm not playing," replied Stitch Head.

"These little snots think they have some claim over my precious cargo," said Freakfinder, pointing to the crate with his cane. "They're thieves, come to steal from your ship, cap'n."

"Take that back, no-neck!" yelled Arabella.

"Thieves, eh?" said the cap'n suspiciously. "We'll see about that. Potts! Chump! Bring them down here, then lock them in the hold."

As the crewmen advanced on them, even Arabella looked nervous.

"What would Captain Flashpowder do?" Stitch Head murmured, his ice-blue eye gleaming like never before.

Stitch Head drew his broken sword and held it above his head. "My name is Stitch Head, and I am a pirate!" he cried.

"I have traveled the ocean wide to take back what is mine! My quarrel is with Fulbert Freakfinder. Return his cargo to me, or face the consequences!"

For a long moment, there was stunned silence aboard the ship. Then laughter rang out across the entire deck.

"Hahaha!"

"Lugs and mumbles, who did you borrow your backbone from?" Freakfinder said with a laugh. "Well, don't just stand there, men — get 'em!"

"You asked for it," said Stitch Head. "Pox! Now!"

Stitch Head looked up into the sails to see Pox perched on the rigging, defiantly still. Stitch Head turned to Arabella. "Uh, would you mind . . . ?"

"No problem," said Arabella with a grin. "Pox! It's feeding time!"

# STITCH HEAD VS. FREAKFINDER

## (Feeding time)

*"An adventure a day
keeps the doctor away!
Unless you get stabbed."*

From
*The Daring Diary of
Captain Flashpowder*

"GRAA–ARHH!" As fast as lightning, Pox swooped down to the crowd of crewmen. He growled madly, biting arms and legs, tearing out hair, and shredding clothes. The panicked crew scattered as the crazed creation attacked them with every ounce of his monstrous fury.

"My eyes!"

"My hair!"

"My ears!" they cried.

"Yes! It's *kick* o'clock!" cried Arabella. She leaped down from the crates and started booting anything that moved.

Stitch Head turned his attention to the crate. He jammed his sword into the lock and tried to pry it open.

"I'll save you ... master!" Stitch Head cried.

"Oh, no, you don't!" Freakfinder said with a growl, scurrying up the crates. "Try to take what's mine, will you?!"

Stitch Head turned around just in time to see Freakfinder swing his cane. Stitch Head ducked. The cane came crashing down on the top of the professor's crate.

"You thieving little snot! I'll knock your head off!" yelled Freakfinder, banging the crate with his cane.

Stitch Head dodged left, then right, desperately avoiding Freakfinder's blows — and found himself balanced precariously on the edge of the stack. He glanced behind him at the long drop into the surging sea.

"Nowhere left for you to run! That'll teach you to play at being pirates," Freakfinder said, sneering. He swung his cane back and forth at Stitch Head.

Stitch Head threw himself at Freakfinder and slid between his legs. He grabbed his wooden sword out of the crate's lock and faced Freakfinder.

"HA! What's that supposed to be?" Freakfinder cackled.

"That," replied Stitch Head firmly, "is my trusty sword. And I'm not playing. I am a pirate."

Stitch Head launched himself at Freakfinder. Sword clashed against cane! Stitch Head felt his tiny bones rattle under the impact.

Freakfinder was so much bigger and stronger than he was. He parried two more blows, but could barely keep hold of his sword — his stitches were strained to the breaking point.

"Hold still!" howled Freakfinder. "Hold still while I bash you!"

But Stitch Head kept moving, weaving in and out of Freakfinder's legs. Before long, Freakfinder began puffing and gasping.

"Hold still, you snot," he growled.

This was Stitch Head's chance! He jumped over the cane and onto the professor's crate.

Then Stitch Head raised his sword.

"Who's out there? Release me, I say!" protested the professor, rattling the crate with all his might. As Stitch Head struggled to keep his footing, Freakfinder lunged with the last of his strength. He struck hard with his cane, knocking Stitch Head's sword out of his hand. It spun and whirled high into the air.

"Not so . . . swashbucklin' now . . . are ya!" stammered Freakfinder. Stitch Head's eye darted upward to his spinning sword. Suddenly, he leaped toward Freakfinder and grabbed him by the ears, then scrambled up his hat until he reached the top. As Freakfinder flailed and cursed, stumbling forward, Stitch Head flipped upward!

As he spun through the air, time itself seemed to slow down. Stitch Head saw the polished wood of the deck, and then the billowing clouds and the white light of the sun.

Then, as he landed back on the crate, he raised his hand — and his still-spinning sword fell right into his fingers.

"Told you it was trusty," whispered Stitch Head. He swung his sword. CLANK! The blow knocked Freakfinder's cane over the side of the ship and into the churning sea.

"Lugs and . . . mumbles!" Freakfinder said between gasps. He gripped his chest and fell to his knees. "You'll give me a . . . . heart attack with all this . . . horseplay!"

Stitch Head's eye glinted in the sunlight. He gently placed his sword under Freakfinder's chin.

"Open that crate and free my master," he said. "Do it. Now!"

"Get off me!" Arabella yelled. "I'll kick your knees off!"

"Arabella?" said Stitch Head. He wheeled around to see the cap'n holding her in midair by her neck. The other crewmen, scarred and chewed from their battle with Pox, had managed to throw a sack over the mad monkey-bat.

"Leave her alone!" Stitch Head cried. "I mean it!"

"I give the orders around here, by criminy!" hollered the cap'n. "Now drop your silly sword and come down from up there!"

"Don't do it, Stitch Head!" screamed Arabella, kicking.

"Hush, you! You nearly broke my shin bone with all that kicking," growled the cap'n, shaking her wildly.

"*No!* Please don't hurt her!" cried Stitch Head, throwing his trusty sword to the deck.

"That's better! Now let's get rid of them!" howled Freakfinder. He grabbed Stitch Head, hoisting him into the air and dangling him over the side of the ship.

"Hang on a minute, Freakfinder," said the cap'n. "No one said anything about drowning children!"

"He's no child . . . he's a monster! A freak! He escaped from a lunatic asylum — just like the old man in the crate!"

"That's a lie!" cried Stitch Head.

"Please, we haven't escaped from anywhere. Freakfinder kidnapped the professor — who is mad, but in a mad professoring sort of way — and he intends to use him to make monsters for his freak show!"

"Lugs and mumbles, you've got a big mouth for a little snot," snarled Freakfinder. "I ain't about to have you ruin my chance at fame and fortune!"

"Freakfinder, *don't* —!" cried the cap'n. But it was too late. Freakfinder hurled Stitch Head into the sea.

# CREATION OVERBOARD
### (Let's play pirates)

"*Overboard is underrated.*"

From
*The Daring Diary of*
*Captain Flashpowder*

"WAAHHH!" screamed Stitch Head as he plummeted toward the ocean. His almost-life flashed before his piratey eye — and he wondered if even Captain Flashpowder would know what to do right now. But, just as he expected to crash into the water . . .

KRUMP!

"Ow!" cried Stitch Head. He'd never fallen into the sea before, but this didn't feel like water at all.

"Welcome ABOARD!" came a wild cry. Stitch Head stared up into the grinning face of the Creature and glanced around in disbelief. He was on the *Gadabout II!*

"Creature!" cried Stitch Head. "You're all right!"

"BETTER than all right!" it boomed, wringing out its waterlogged coat. "I discovered I'm the BESTEST SWIMMER ever! I'm like a big MERMAID! Or

Mer-CREATURE. Did you know I have GILLS? They're GREAT! So there I was, practicing my DOGGY-PADDLE, when I came across the *GADABOUT II* in the water! And since you weren't in it . . ."

"Creature, you're amazing!" cried Stitch Head.

"All in a day's PIRATING, Captain Stitch Head!" it said, saluting him.

Stitch Head saluted back, and then pointed up at the big ship.

"Speaking of pirates," said Stitch Head, "we still need to rescue the rest of our trusty crew."

"GREAT!" cried the Creature, scooping Stitch Head up in its third hand and leaping from the *Gadabout II*. It dug its free hands into the thick wood of the ship's hull and began climbing the side. It reached the top in seconds, and then tossed itself onto the deck.

"AARRG! BEWARE, ye LAND-LUBBERS!" it roared, waving its three arms and tail. "I'm in a PIRATEY MOOD!"

All of the crewmen froze in place. "*MONSTER!*" screamed one.

"Actually, it's *CREATURE*," Creature replied. "Until I think of a BETTER name, that is . . . ARR!"

The crewmen's shrill screams filled the air as they scattered in terror!

"HEY, everyone's REALLY getting into CHARACTER," the Creature said excitedly. It placed Stitch Head on the deck. "NOW I'd better DO something *really* PIRATEY."

The Creature roared its most impressive "YAARRRR!" yet and began chasing the crewmen around the ship, crying, "I'll SHIVER your TIMBERS!"

"Go get 'em," cried Stitch Head, grabbing his sword off the deck.

"Criminy, this be madness!" wailed the cap'n, dropping Arabella. She immediately kicked him hard in the shin. THUMP! He crumpled to the ground.

"Stitch Head! You ain't looking half as drowned as I thought you would," said Arabella, watching the Creature chase the terrified crewmen around the deck.

Stitch Head looked up at the crates. His master's crate was still there, but . . .

"Where's Freakfinder?" Stitch Head whispered.

"Lugs and mumbles, don't let it get me!" came the terrified cry. Stitch Head looked up and up . . . until he spotted Freakfinder climbing the rigging. He clambered all the way up and wrapped his spindly arms round the nearest mast.

"Allow me," said Arabella. She pulled open the sack containing the growling, thrashing Pox and released him. Pox shook with rage and looked for something to bite. Arabella pointed at the mast and grinned.

"Go get that bad man," Arabella commanded her trusty companion. "That's right, my lovely monkey-bat!"

# THE TWENTY-FOURTH CHAPTER

# RESCUING THE MAD PROFESSOR

## (The cap'n's favorite book)

> *"Invest in adventure!"*
>
> From
> *The Daring Diary of*
> *Captain Flashpowder*

It wasn't long before Stitch Head and his trusty crew had taken over the ship. Pox quickly dislodged Fulbert Freakfinder from the mast, sending him crashing to the deck with an almighty KRU-DUMP! The Creature dumped him with the cap'n and crew. They all huddled and trembled on the deck in fear.

"That was GREAT!" boomed the Creature, looming over the sailors. Pox flapped around them, snapping his jaws. "Being a PIRATE is SO much better than going to TEA PARTIES! YAARRRR!"

Stitch Head and Arabella climbed back up to the crates. They pried open the top one.

YOINK! The professor popped out like a jack-in-the-box, flailing frantically.

"Foul villainy! Beastly fiends! I am kidnapped! You cannot keep me from my laboratory! I have creations simmering!"

"Master, it's all right. You're safe now," said Stitch Head. "It's *me!* Stitch Head."

"Who?" asked the professor again.

"Oh, for goodness' sake! Back in your box, you ungrateful, old nut!" said Arabella, slamming the lid on the professor.

"Arabella! What are you doing?" cried Stitch Head.

"I reckon if a mad professor don't even recognize his first creation, he don't deserve no fresh air," she said. "He'll be all right in there for a while. After all, do *you* want to be the one tell the prof that he ain't got no award waiting for him?"

"Um, I suppose not," replied Stitch Head. He gave a faint smile and breathed a long, slow sigh of relief. His master was safe — and that was good enough for now.

"So WHAT should we DO with *THEM?*" asked the Creature, striking its most piratey pose in front of the terrified crew. "Oooo! Let's make them WALK the PLANK! NOTHING'S more PIRATE-LIKE than PLANK-walking . . ."

"Please don't hurt us!" cried the cap'n. "We are but humble sailors, trying to make an honest living!"

"Ain't nothing honest about kidnapping a crazy, old geezer," said Arabella.

"We were led astray by Freakfinder. Now we know he ain't no friend of ours!" cried the cap'n.

"Lugs and mumbles, I want my money back, you backstabbing pirate scum!" grumbled Freakfinder.

"We can't listen to this all day — we've got a world of adventure ahead of us," said Arabella. "Let's make 'em swim home with their shoes on. That's the pirate's way. That's what Captain Flashpowder would do!"

"Captain . . . Flashpowder?" repeated the cap'n. "*You* know Captain Flashpowder?"

Stitch Head's eye glinted in the midday sun. "Do — do you?" he replied.

"Of course! It be my favorite storybook!" cried the cap'n. "Why, it's the book that made me want to be a sea captain. I've read it over a hundred times!"

"Storybook . . . ?" whispered Stitch Head, climbing down the crates to the deck.

"Aye! To adventure, and all that! See, you can't make me walk the plank! We have so much in common!" continued the cap'n hopefully.

The cap'n reached into his coat and groped around. "I still take it everywhere with me!"

Stitch Head watched in amazement as the cap'n pulled a book out of his coat pocket. It was battered and torn, but he recognized it immediately.

It was *The Daring Diary of Captain Flashpowder.*

# THE TWENTY-FIFTH CHAPTER

# ONWARD
## (The truth about Captain Flashpowder)

*"Adventure is in the eye
of the beholder."*

From
*The Daring Diary of
Captain Flashpowder*

I don't understand," whispered Stitch Head, staring at the book in the cap'n's hand. "Captain Flashpowder's diary . . . it's still in Castle Grotteskew. How could you have it?"

"There wasn't a boy in my hometown who didn't have a copy of *The Daring Diary of Captain Flashpowder* — but no one loved it as much as me, by criminy!" continued the cap'n. "So, does this mean we be friends now? *Book buddies!* You wouldn't make a fellow Flashpowder fan walk the plank, would you?"

As Stitch Head peered at the cap'n's book, the truth slowly dawned on him. *The Daring Diary of Captain Flashpowder* wasn't a diary at all. It was a storybook. It was all just a story. He felt his borrowed blood run cold.

"But that means . . ." he murmured, holding his tiny hand up to his pirate's eye. "Flashpowder's not *real?*"

"I wish he were, by criminy! The world would be a more exciting place," replied the cap'n. "Still, we can always imagine, can't we?"

"Ha! You thought you were part pirate? Part Flashpowder?" Freakfinder said with a laugh. "Lugs and mumbles, what a joke!"

"Shut your cake-hole, dog-face!" growled Arabella. "Unless you want Pox to eat your mustache!"

Stitch Head pulled the eyepatch off his head. Freakfinder was right. If Captain Flashpowder wasn't real, then his remarkable, ice-blue eye was just an eye, and nothing more.

"I'm not a pirate," he whispered. "I'm not even *part* pirate."

"Oh, Stitch Head . . ." said the Creature. "I was so SURE you *were!*"

Stitch Head slumped onto the deck. He felt as if he'd been tricked. Or perhaps, he had just seen what he wanted to see.

Perhaps Stitch Head been fooling himself all along.

"That don't mean nothing!" shouted Arabella, scurrying down from the crates. "Eye or no eye, *you* built a ship and *you* set sail! *You* drew your sword and took over this whole ship and saved that reptile-faced master of yours! I ain't never seen more pirate-like behavior in all my days! I don't care whose eyes you got, Stitch Head — ain't no one can take away what you did."

Stitch Head slowly looked up. He glanced with both eyes out at the shimmering ocean. It still looked as glorious as it did when he first put on the eyepatch and saw the world of adventure in his mind's eye. He may not be part pirate after all, but Arabella was right. Something in him had changed. *He* had changed.

"The professor belongs in Castle Grotteskew. And he always will," said Stitch Head. He turned to the cap'n. "If we let you go, will you take us back to the harbor, please?"

"Aye! Whatever you say," replied the cap'n. Then he pointed to Freakfinder. "And what about this fiend?"

"Make him walk the plank!" snapped Arabella. "See how he likes swimming with the fishes!"

"Do your worst!" said Freakfinder. "I'm not scared of no *freaks.*"

Stitch Head stared at Freakfinder.

"Let him go, too," Stitch Head finally said. "If he's brave enough to go anywhere near Castle Grotteskew again, I'll be waiting for him."

"We'll all be waiting — boots at the ready!" growled Arabella. Then she turned to face Stitch Head. "But . . . do you really want to go back, Stitch Head? The professor might belong in the castle . . . but what about *you?*"

"YEAH, what about *our* GREAT ADVENTURE?" said the Creature.

"YaBBiT!" yapped Pox in agreement.

"I think I've had enough adventure for today," replied Stitch Head. He looked out to sea. "But there's always tomorrow."

First published in the United States in 2013
by Capstone Young Readers
A Capstone Imprint
1710 Roe Crest Drive
North Mankato, Minnesota 56003
www.capstonepub.com

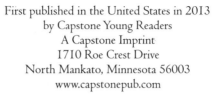

First published by
Stripes Publishing
1 The Coda Centre, 189 Munster Road
London SW6 6AW

Text copyright © Guy Bass, 2011
Illustrations copyright © Pete Williamson, 2011

All Rights Reserved

Library of Congress Cataloging-in-Publication Data is available
on the Library of Congress website.

ISBN: 978-1-62370-008-9

Summary:
Mad Professor Erasmus has long forgotten his first creation, Stitch
Head, leaving the lonely patchwork monster to take care of Castle
Grotteskew all by himself. But when the professor is kidnapped by
crusty pirates, Stitch Head decides to risk his almost-life to save
his creator. But he'll need a little help from his new friends, the
Creature and Arabella, to learn to embrace his inner pirate.

Printed in China.
032013    007228RRDF13